Book 8

THE NEW KID ON JUPITER

BY JEFF DINARDO
ILLUSTRATED BY DAVE CLEGG

RED CHAIR
PRESS

Funny Bone Books

and Funny Bone Readers are produced and published by

Red Chair Press LLC   PO Box 333   South Egremont, MA 01258-0333

www.redchairpress.com

About the Author

Jeff Dinardo's books are filled with humor and silliness that captures a child's imagination. When not writing, Jeff runs a successful design firm specializing in textbooks for use in classrooms from K-8.

About the Artist

Dave Clegg lives and works on a small horse farm in north Georgia with his wife Lyn and their two children. All of Dave's work is done digitally on his computer. When he is not drawing, he can be found creating songs with his guitar or making robot sculptures!

Publisher's Cataloging-In-Publication Data

Names: Dinardo, Jeffrey. | Clegg, Dave, illustrator. | Dinardo, Jeffrey. Jupiter twins ; bk. 8.
Title: The new kid on Jupiter / by Jeff Dinardo ; illustrated by Dave Clegg.
Other Titles: Funny bone books. First chapters.

Description: South Egremont, MA : Red Chair Press, [2019] | Interest age level: 005-007. | Summary: "There's a new kid in school. Will he be a good team player at Field Day or will he drag down the fun? Find out how the Twins make him feel welcome."--Provided by publisher.

Identifiers: ISBN 9781634407533 (library hardcover) | ISBN 9781634407571 (paperback) | ISBN 9781634407618 (ebook)

Subjects: LCSH: Twins--Juvenile fiction. | Jupiter (Planet)--Juvenile fiction. | Outer space--Exploration--Juvenile fiction. | Students--Juvenile fiction. | CYAC: Twins--Fiction. | Jupiter (Planet)--Fiction. | Outer space--Exploration--Fiction. | Students--Fiction.

Classification: LCC PZ7.D6115 Juk 2019 (print) | LCC PZ7.D6115 (ebook) | DDC [E]--dc23 | LCCN: 2018955674

Printed in United States of America

0519 1P CGF19

CONTENTS

Meet the Characters

Trudy

Tina

Ms. Bickleblorb

Bobby

Beep, *Beep, Beep* went the alarm.

Trudy groggily woke and hit the snooze button.

"I was having a dream about eating giant blueberries," she said.

Her twin sister Tina looked at the clock.

"*Jumping Jupiter!*" she said. "We are going to miss the space bus!"

The girls quickly got dressed and ran downstairs.

"About time, girls," said their mother.

Their father gave them each a nutrient bar.

"You better hurry or the space bus will take off without you," he said.

The girls grabbed the food and ran out of the door.

The space bus was waiting for them.

"Of all days to be late!" said Tina.

"I know," said Trudy. "It's Field Day!"

Field Day was when all the kids in their school competed against each other in games like sonic ping pong, laser sprinting and jet pack jumping.

Trudy was the school's best ping-pong player, and she had won the tournament the last three years in a row.

"No one can beat me!" she thought.

When the space bus landed, all the kids got out.

"Field Day, Field Day!" they were all chanting.

As Trudy ran up the steps she saw a new student who was walking all alone.

He didn't look like anyone else on Jupiter.

He was round and squishy, and you could almost see right through him.

Trudy thought he didn't seem very happy.

"Come on," said Tina as she grabbed her sister. "We can't be late for class."

THE NEW KID

"Good morning, class," said their teacher Ms. Bickleblorb. "As you all know, today is Field Day."

All the class cheered.

"Quiet, please," Ms. Bickleblorb continued. "But first we have some regular schoolwork to do."

The kids groaned.

Ms. Bickleblorb grabbed some papers from her desk and handed them out.

"I graded your reports on The Martian moon landing," she said. "And some of you did extremely well."

She handed Tina her report. It had an "A+" on the top.

Just then the school's principal came into the classroom. He was walking with the new kid that Trudy had seen.

The principal talked to Ms. Bickleblorb for a minute, then he left. The new kid stayed. He stared at the ground. Trudy thought he seemed sad.

"Class," said their teacher, "we have a new student joining us. This is Bobby."

"He looks more like a *blobby*," said one of the boys behind Tina.

Ms. Bickleblorb ignored the rude remark.

"Bobby and his family just moved here from Triton, one of the moons of Neptune."

Bobby just looked around but didn't say anything. He shimmied over to the empty seat in the back of the room and sat down.

It was finally time for Field Day, and all the kids ran outside.

"I can't wait for the ping-pong tournament to start," said Trudy.

Tina saw Bobby squiggle by and sit on a bench by himself.

One boy ran up to Bobby and intentionally bumped into him.

"Hey, he jiggles!" the boy laughed before running away.

The twins scowled at the boy.

Trudy got up and walked over to Bobby.

"Come sit with us," she said.

Bobby looked around the field.

"I miss my old school," he said. "No one here is like me."

Trudy pointed to her left leg.

"I am the only one in school with one wheel," she said. "We can both be different together."

Bobby looked at her wheel.

"That's cool!" he said with a smile.

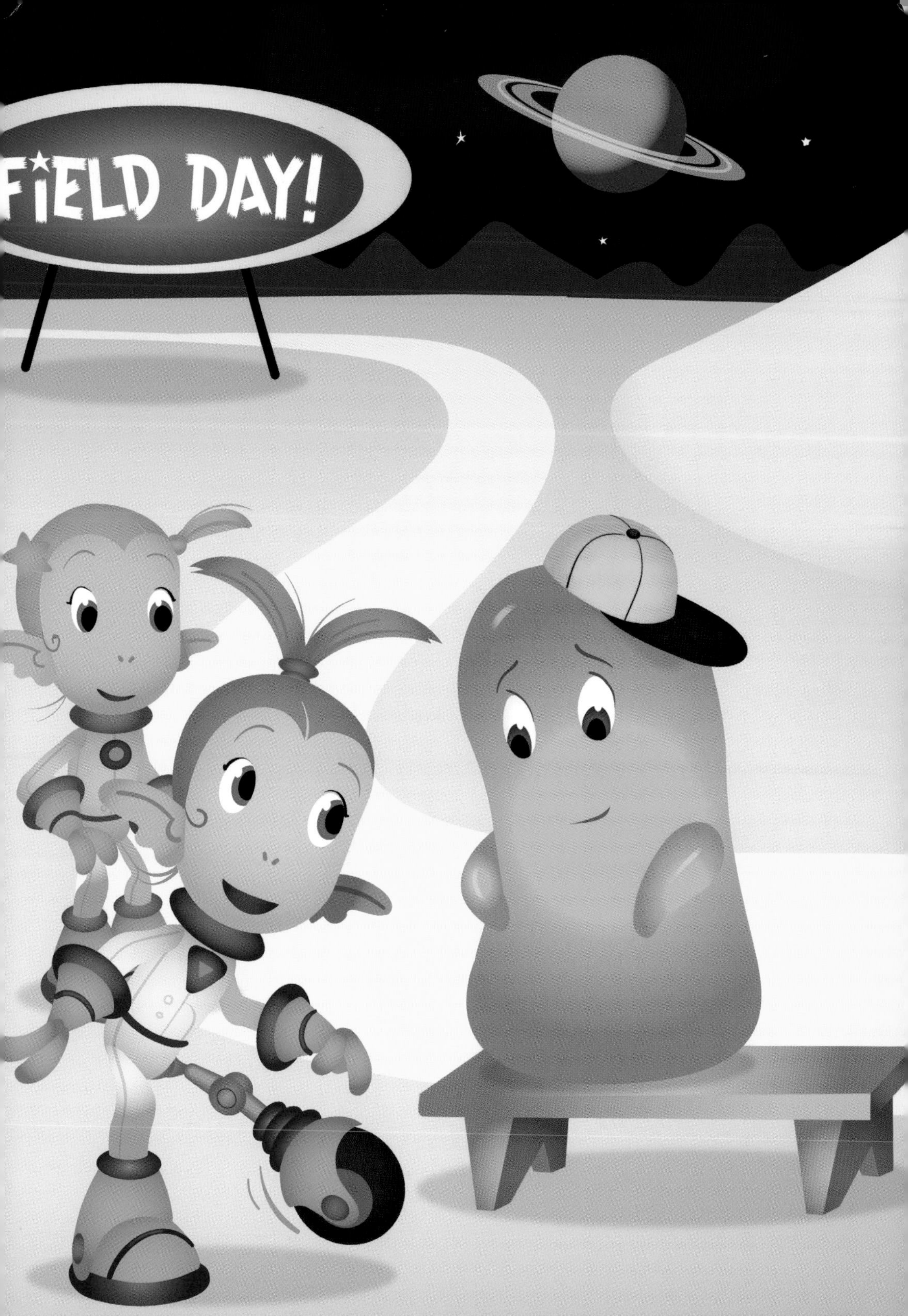
FIELD DAY!

3 FIELD DAY

Field day started.

All the kids took turns running, jumping and playing different games.

Tina came in third place during laser sprinting.

It was almost time for sonic ping-pong, and Trudy was practicing her shots.

"Oh, we play this game on Triton!" said Bobby. "Can I help you practice?"

Trudy served the ball to Bobby and he rocketed the ball right back. It was a perfect shot.

"Wow, you are good!" said Trudy.

She served it again and Bobby hit
another perfect shot in the corner.
They practiced together for a long time.
Many of the kids watched them.

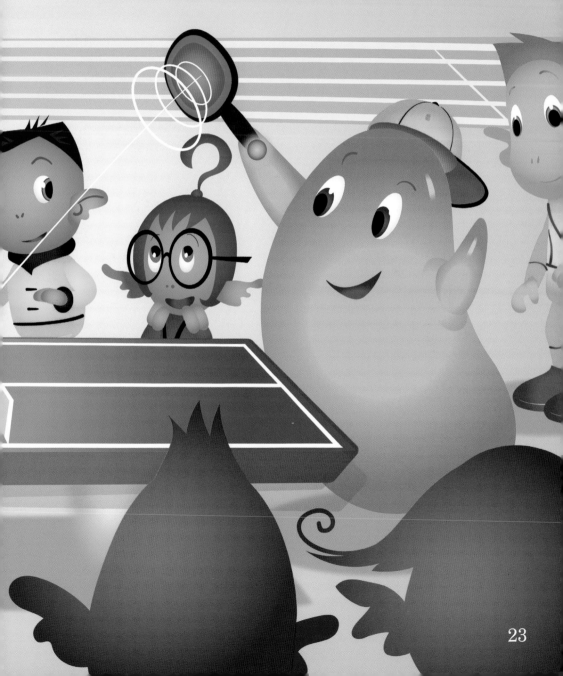

Ms. Bickleblorb had watched them practice too.

"Bobby, you really play well," she said. "So I signed you up for the tournament too!"

"Hurray," all the kids cheered.

Trudy was not so happy.

"I don't want to beat my new friend," she told her sister.

"Well, it would be nice if Bobby won," said Tina. "The other kids might stop calling him Blobby."

Trudy just made a face.

The tournament started.

Trudy played several matches. She won each game easily.

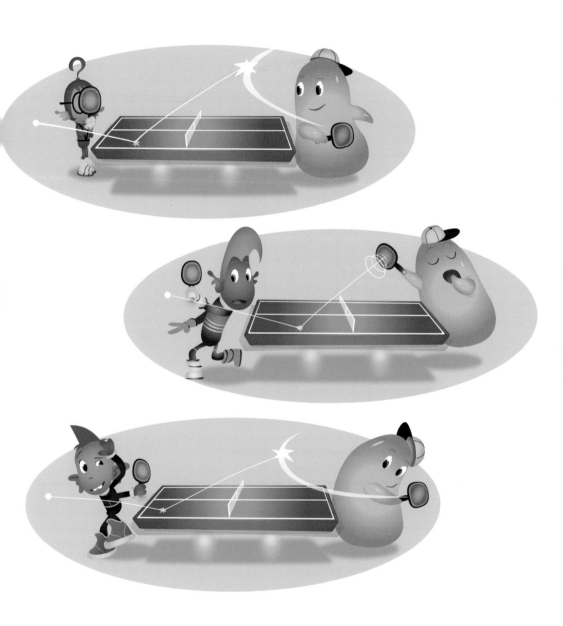

Bobby played several matches too.
He also won easily.

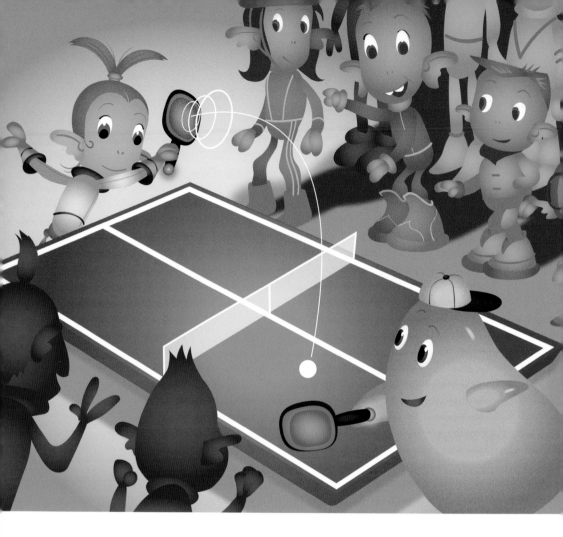

It was the final game to see who would win the tournament.

And it was Trudy against Bobby.

First Trudy scored a point. Then Bobby scored a point.

Then Trudy, then Bobby again.

Back and forth and forth and back.

Bobby got ahead, and if he made one more point he would win the tournament.

He looked at Trudy.

"I know what this means to you," he whispered. "Do you want me to lose the game?"

Trudy looked at Bobby. She looked at her sister and at the crowd cheering them both on.

"No thanks," she said back. "Let's play it for real."

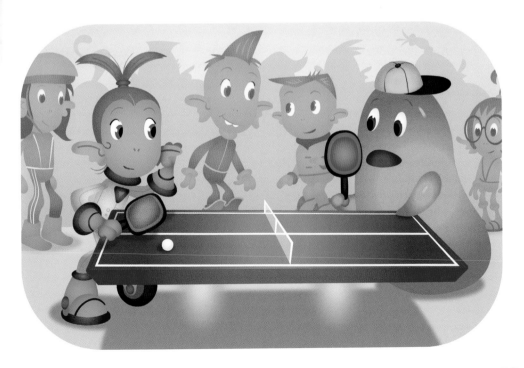

Bobby served a super-fast serve right to the corner.

Trudy got to it in time and zoomed the ball back over the net.

Bobby just got to it and made a spinning shot to the opposite corner.

But Trudy missed the ball when she tried to return it.

Bobby had won.

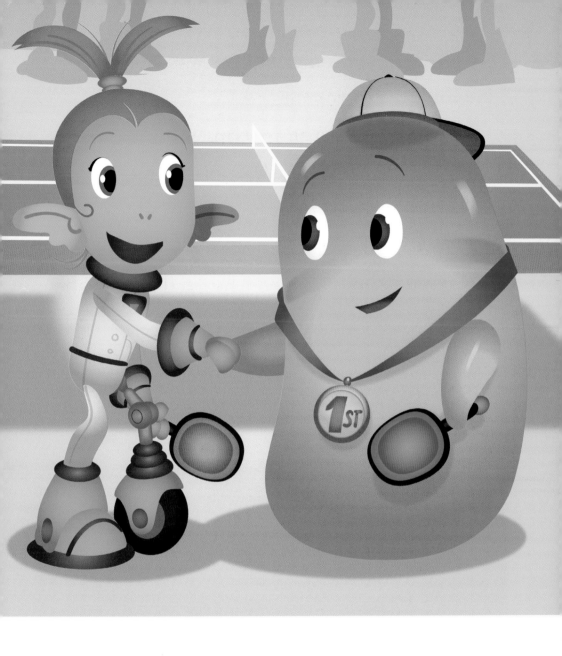

All the kids cheered.

Trudy congratulated Bobby.

"Thanks," he said. "I still miss my
old school, but now I miss it a bit less."

After school, the twins walked home together.

"I know you wanted to win," said Tina. "But I think Bobby was very happy."

Trudy smiled.

"It was fine," she said. "But I only have one year until the next Field Day. I have to start practicing!"

Then Trudy grabbed her sister and ran all the way home.